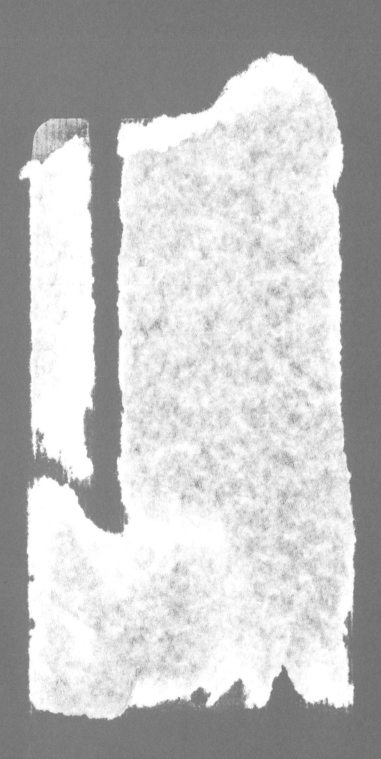

Baby Bear's

Bedtime Book

Written by JANE YOLEN

Illustrated by JANE DYER

Harcourt Brace Jovanovich, Publishers

San Diego   New York   London

To B.B. and her Renaissance Angel

Text copyright © 1990 by Jane Yolen
Illustrations copyright © 1990 by Jane Dyer

Library of Congress Cataloging-in-Publication Data
Yolen, Jane.
Baby Bear's bedtime book/by Jane Yolen; pictures by Jane Dyer.
p. cm.
Summary: Goldilocks tells Baby Bear several bedtime stories: one
silly, one scary, one sad, one angry, one funny, and one of adventure.
ISBN 0-15-205120-1
[1. Animals — Fiction. 2. Bedtime — Fiction.] I. Dyer, Jane, ill.
II. Title.
PZ7.Y78Bab   1990
[E] — dc19   89-2161

First edition   A B C D E

The illustrations in this book were done in colored pencils
and Luma Dyes on 140-lb. Waterford hot press watercolor paper.
The display type was set in Windsor Light
and the text type was set in Adroit Light.
Composition by Thompson Type, San Diego, California
Color separations were made by Bright Arts, Ltd., Hong Kong.
Printed and bound by Tien Wah Press, Singapore
Production supervision by Warren Wallerstein and Ginger Boyer
Designed by Camilla Filancia

"Tell me a story, Goldie," Baby Bear said as they climbed the stairs to his room. "Then I'll go right to bed."

"Only one?" asked Goldie.

"Only one," Baby Bear promised.

They sat on Baby Bear's bed.

"Silly, sad, scary, or funny?" asked Goldie.

"Silly," said Baby Bear.

So Goldie began:

"Once upon a time there were three bears, and they lived in a little cottage deep, deep in the woods —"

"That's not a *silly* story," interrupted Baby Bear. "That's a *true* story. I want a *silly* story."

"What do you consider a *silly* story?" asked Goldie.

"A story about . . ." Baby Bear thought and thought. Then he saw his stuffed elephant on the chair. "A story about an elephant! Elephants are very silly."

"Elephants are only silly to baby bears," said Goldie.

But she began:

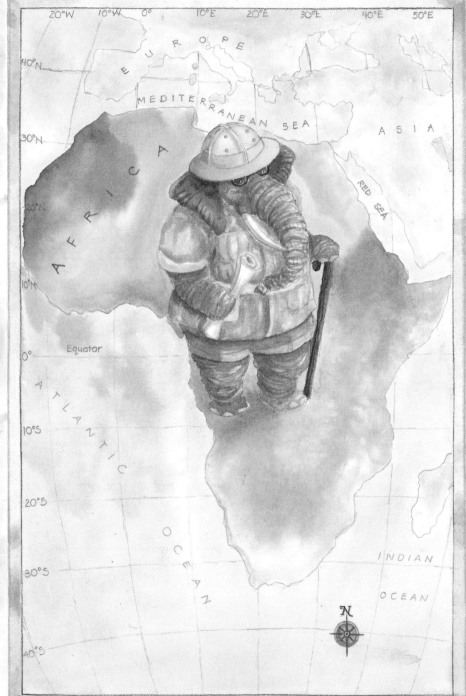

Once upon a time there was an elephant named Morris who lived in Africa. Morris loved to travel.

One day he packed his trunk with everything he would need on his trip: money, clean socks, a freshly ironed handkerchief, a toothbrush, toothpaste, and his favorite book. He packed his trunk so tightly he could scarcely breathe.

Then he went off down the road: *a-trompety-tromp, a-trompety-tromp.*

Pretty soon he came to Bombay where he spent most of his money on spicy food. Then he went to Paris, where he wore out his clean socks. In London, he lost his handkerchief waving it at the queen. He used up his toothbrush and toothpaste in New York City, cleaning his tusks. After he read his book in San Francisco, he gave it to a little boy who had no books of his own. Then he spent the last of his money for a boat ride home.

So you see, there was nothing left in his trunk by the time he got back to Africa. Nothing at all.

When he landed, Morris took a deep, deep breath.

"Travel is lots of fun," he said. "But I always breathe better when I am home. I wonder why?"

"I know why!" cried Baby Bear. "Because he kept so much in his trunk and—"

"Silly stories don't need explanations," said Goldie. "It spoils the fun. And now it is time for bed."

"Going to bed is what spoils the fun," grumped Baby Bear. "Why don't you tell me another story?"

Goldie shook her head.

"Please," begged Baby Bear.

"Only one," said Goldie.

"A scary one," said Baby Bear. "About . . ." He looked around his room. "About a mole."

"Moles aren't scary," said Goldie. "Not even to baby bears."

"About a mole who is scared," Baby Bear explained.

So Goldie began:

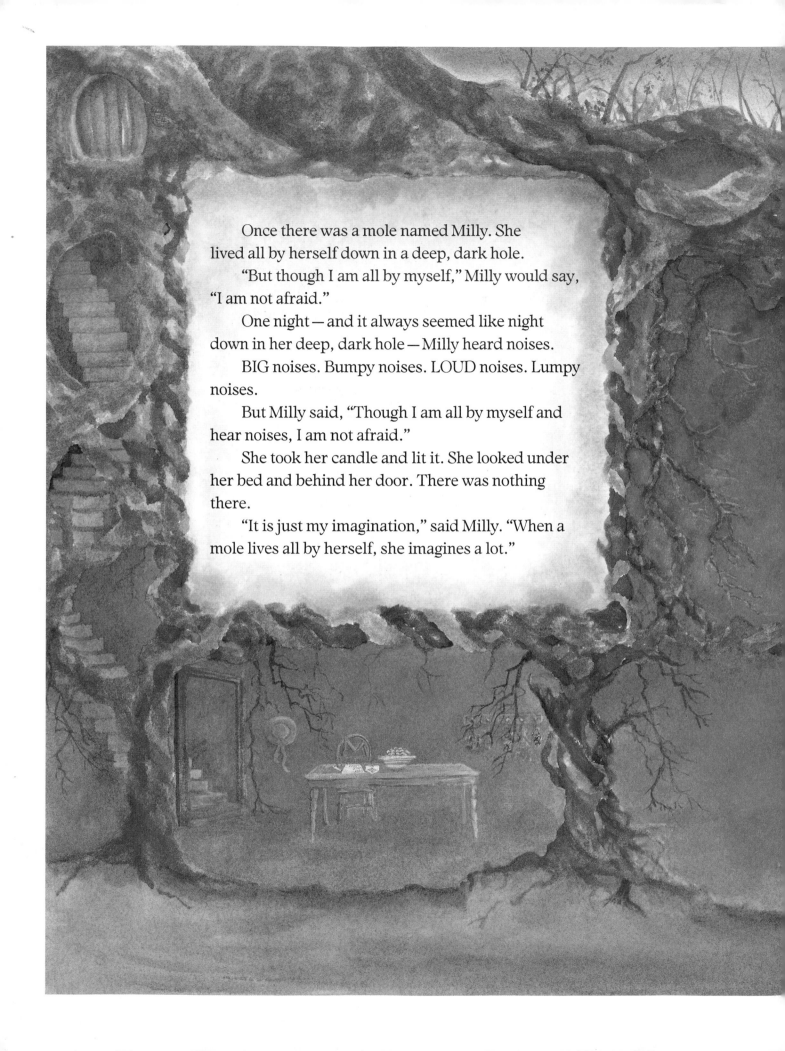

Once there was a mole named Milly. She lived all by herself down in a deep, dark hole.

"But though I am all by myself," Milly would say, "I am not afraid."

One night — and it always seemed like night down in her deep, dark hole — Milly heard noises.

BIG noises. Bumpy noises. LOUD noises. Lumpy noises.

But Milly said, "Though I am all by myself and hear noises, I am not afraid."

She took her candle and lit it. She looked under her bed and behind her door. There was nothing there.

"It is just my imagination," said Milly. "When a mole lives all by herself, she imagines a lot."

So she went back to bed, blew out her candle, and closed her eyes.

The noises began again. BIG noises. Bumpy noises. LOUD noises. Lumpy noises. HIGH noises. Scritchy noises. LOW noises. Scratchy noises.

She pulled the covers over her head. She pulled the pillow over her head. And then she remembered that though she was all by herself, she was not afraid. So she took the pillow off her head. She took the covers off her head. She reached for the candle and . . . *somebody* put the candle in her hand.

"I am *not* by myself," thought Milly. "*Not* at all. So why am I suddenly so very much afraid?"

"I know! I know why she's afraid!" Baby Bear
cried out. "But who put the candle in her hand?"

"Scary stories don't need explanations," said
Goldie. "It spoils the fun. Time for sleep."

"Going to sleep is what really spoils the fun,"
growled Baby Bear. "Tell me one more story, Goldie."

"No more stories," said Goldie firmly.

"Please," begged Baby Bear.

"Only one," said Goldie.

"Only one," said Baby Bear. "A sad story.
About . . ." He looked around his room. "About an
anteater."

"Anteaters aren't sad," said Goldie.

"They are to baby bears," said Baby Bear.

So Goldie began:

There was once a very sad anteater named Uncle Aldo. He was sad because he ate ants. And you would be sad, too, if you ate nothing but ants. When they get into your tummy, they hop around doing ant dances like the shimmy and the shammy, the tarantella and the shag.

Because his tummy was filled with ant dances all day long, poor Uncle Aldo always had a tummyache. And that, as you can imagine, made him very sad indeed.

Uncle Aldo went to a different doctor every day of the week. They gave him medicines in bottles and medicines in boxes; medicines that began with the letter W and medicines that began with the letter M. They gave him pills and lotions, needles and potions. They suggested hot packs, and cold packs, and long, luke-warm baths.

But nothing helped.

His tummy continued to jump around and bump around with ant dances like the castle rock and the bunny hop, the turkey trot and the twist.

Finally, in desperation, Uncle Aldo decided to learn to dance himself.

"Because if you can't beat 'em, join 'em," became his motto.

He learned to do the shimmy and the shammy, the tarantella and the shag. He learned the castle rock and the bunny hop, the turkey trot and the twist. His insteps hurt as much as his insides, so he couldn't sleep at night.

But in his third dance lesson he learned to waltz. It was wonderful. *One-two-three, glide-two-three. One-two-three, slide-two-three.* Smooth and flowing.

The next morning he taught it to the ants, right before he ate them. They waltzed right into his tummy, *one-two-three, glide-two-three. One-two-three, slide-two-three.*

Waltzing became the most popular dance in the ant kingdom. They had contests for waltz king and queen.

And Uncle Aldo never had a tummyache again because his meals were always smooth. And flowing.

"That isn't a sad story," said Baby Bear.

"It is if you're an ant!" replied Goldie. "Now, time for bed."

"*That's* a sad story if you're a baby bear," said Baby Bear. "Tell me one more."

"No," said Goldie.

"Please," begged Baby Bear.

"No!" said Goldie.

"If you do, I'll go right to sleep," said Baby Bear.

"Only one?" asked Goldie.

"An angry story," said Baby Bear. "About . . ." He looked around. "About an alligator."

"Alligators aren't angry," said Goldie.

"They are to baby bears," said Baby Bear.

So Goldie began:

Once there was an alligator named Arnold who lived in an old army truck in the middle of the Amazon River.

He only liked things beginning with the letter A.

He had an armchair and he had an abacus on which he counted his money.

When he was hungry he ate acorns, apples, and albacore, which is a kind of tuna fish.

At night, before he went to bed, he played his accordion.

And when he wanted to fall asleep, he didn't count sheep jumping over fences. He counted alpacas arching over anchors. It made him snore until morning.

Now, all would have been "Absolutely Amazing and Altogether All right," as Arnold liked to say, except that one day, by accident, a box fell out of a passing airplane.

The box was marked: DEFECTIVE, RETURN TO SENDER, which meant there was something wrong with what was inside.

Arnold opened the box and found it contained alphabet blocks. Every letter was there but . . .

"NO A!" shouted Arnold, who was Absolutely and Amazingly Altogether Angry. "This box certainly *is* defective."

He threw the box into the Amazon River. But the blocks were made of wood, so they floated. They bumped into his army truck. They scared away the albacore. They even kept the alpacas from arching over anchors in Arnold's dreams.

Arnold was so Altogether Angry, he gathered up the blocks, tied them together into a raft, and, using a long pole, made his way down the Amazon until he came to the sea.

There he found a big city, where he sold the alphabet raft to an odd millionaire. He had his picture taken with astronauts and actors, and he wrote a book about his adventures. He called it *The Story of A by Arnold Alligator.*

With the money he made, he bought twenty-six sets of alphabet blocks. He took out all the A's and made another raft. He paddled back up the Amazon to his old army truck.

And there he lived, Absolutely and Amazingly Altogether 'Appily ever After.

"Not *Happily* ever after?" asked Baby Bear.

"No," said Goldie, "because *Happily* begins with an H, and Arnold didn't like H's. Only A's."

"Angry stories don't need explanations," said Baby Bear. "But baby bears need one more story."

"No, they don't," said Goldie.

"Only one?" begged Baby Bear.

"Only one," said Goldie, giving in.

"A funny story about . . ." He looked around. "About a sheep."

"Sheep *are* funny," said Goldie.

"Especially to baby bears," said Baby Bear.

So Goldie began:

There was once a flock of sheep, and every single one of them was named Sam. Even the girls.

They all had the same name, and they all looked alike. In fact they looked so much alike they were not sure how many of them were in the flock.

Every time they tried to count themselves, they got mixed up. They tried counting noses, and they tried counting tails. They tried counting eyes and dividing by two. They tried counting legs and dividing by four. Some days they counted twelve, and some days they counted nine. Some days they counted a zillion seventy. They were very sad.

"This is a baaaaad situation," said one Sam, who considered herself the flock's leader.

"We need help baaaaaadly," said another Sam, who saw to it that they got home to the pen safely every night.

1 · 2 · 3 · 4 · 5 ·

So all the Sams wrote a letter to a counting company in the city: *J. Alfred Collie & Sons*. The company sent the youngest son out to count the sheep because he needed the most practice.

He counted them once. Then he counted them again. When he was sure he was right, he gave them his bill.

"There are ten sheep," he said. "Ten noses and ten tails. Twenty eyes and forty feet." He smiled a toothy smile and went home.

Sam, the best adder-upper, added up all the numbers. "Ten plus ten plus ten plus twenty plus forty equals ninety. That's almost one hundred," he said.

From that day on, if anyone asked the flock how many Sams there were, they always said, "Almost one hundred." And they were always almost right. It made them very happy.

·6· 7· 8· 9·10

"Very happy and very silly!" shouted Baby Bear. "That was so silly, I need another story." He yawned.

"No," said Goldie. "Time for bed."

"Only one," begged Baby Bear, rubbing his eyes. "Only one?"

"A big adventure story about . . ." He looked around. "About a tiger."

"Tigers do have exciting adventures," agreed Goldie. "Especially with baby bears."

So she began:

There was once a tiger the color of sand and weeds who lived in a cave in the Cinnabar Hills. He had no mother and no father. And worst of all, he had no name.

One night, he looked around and said, "Trees have names. A cave has a name. Stars have names. The moon has a name. But I have no one to give a name to me."

So the very next day he decided to go looking for a name.

He walked and walked until he came to a meadow where a flock of sheep were grazing on the grass.

"Hello, sheep," said the tiger. "I am looking for a name."

The sheep looked up. "Our name is Sam," they said. "You could be Sam, too."

The tiger shook his head. "That is not a tiger's name."

He went a little farther and came to a big river where an alligator was sitting in an army truck playing an accordion.

"Hello, alligator," said the tiger. "I am looking for a name."

The alligator stopped playing his accordion, right between *do* and *re*. "You could be called Arnold," he said. "Or Adam. Or Alloysius. Or Alice — though that is a girl's name. Are you a girl?"

"I am a tiger," said the tiger, "and those are not the names for me."

He went a little farther and came to an anthill where ants were dancing up and down. By the side of the hill was an anteater humming a waltz.

"Hello, anteater," said the tiger. "I am looking for a name."

The anteater stopped humming between one beat and the next. "My name is Uncle Aldo," he said. "You could borrow that for a while. Just for as long as it takes me to waltz these ants into my tummy."

"I am not an uncle," said the tiger. "And I am not an aunt."

"Lucky for you," said Uncle Aldo. "If you were an ant I would have to eat you." He began humming again.

Shaking his head, the tiger went on. He came to a deep, dark hole. He got down on his knees and looked in. There were two moles side by side on a bed reading a book together.

"Hello, moles," said the tiger. "I am looking for a name."

"My name is Milly," said one mole.

"My name is Moley," said the other.

They smiled at one another.

The tiger shook his head. "I am neither a mill nor a mole," he said. "So those are not my names." He went on.

He came to an African thatched hut with a big sign on the door. Taking out his glasses, he read:

Gone traveling. Home soon. No newspapers till further notice.

Love, Morris Elephant

"That's a good name for an elephant," said the tiger. "But not for me."

At last he came to a cozy cottage in the woods. He knocked on the door. When no one answered, he walked right in.

There was a table set with three bowls of porridge. One was too hot. One was too cold. And one was just right. . . .

"Wait," said Baby Bear, "I know *that* story. But I want to know the end of the other one. Does the tiger ever get his name?"

"What do you think?" asked Goldie.

Baby Bear picked up his special tiger. He gave it a hug. "I think he met Baby Bear and Baby Bear gave him a name. Baby Bear called him Friend Tiger."

"So he did," said Goldie. "And that's the end of the story."

"Tell me one more," said Baby Bear.

Goldie shook her head.

"Tell me a *true* story," begged Baby Bear. He snuggled under the quilt with Friend Tiger.

"Well, just this very last story," said Goldie. "But no more."

So she began:

Once upon a time, in a little cottage in the woods
there lived three bears. There was Mama Bear and
Papa Bear and little Baby Bear.

One day . . .

But she didn't have to go any farther, because
Baby Bear wasn't listening. He was fast asleep.